This book is given with love
To:

_____

From:

_____

About the Author

Dr. Daniela Owen is a psychologist who brings to life healthy mind concepts and strategies for children everywhere. For more about the author please check out

drdanielaowen.com

For Lila Skye

EVERYONE FEELS
ANXIOUS
SOMETIMES

Written by:
Dr. Daniela Owen

Illustrated by:
Gülce Baycik

Lots of different things
can make us feel **anxious...**

Like being in new situations,
performing in front of others,
or competing in sports.

We can also feel anxious
when we're running late,
meeting people for the first time,
or playing a game that
we're not very good at.

Feeling anxious may make us
want to run away as *fast* as we can...

Or it may make us freeze up,
feel like we can't move,
or sometimes like we can't even speak.

Anxiety can even make us act **angry** and cause us to kick, scream, push, cry, or break things.

It can make our bodies feel bad
in all kinds of different ways...

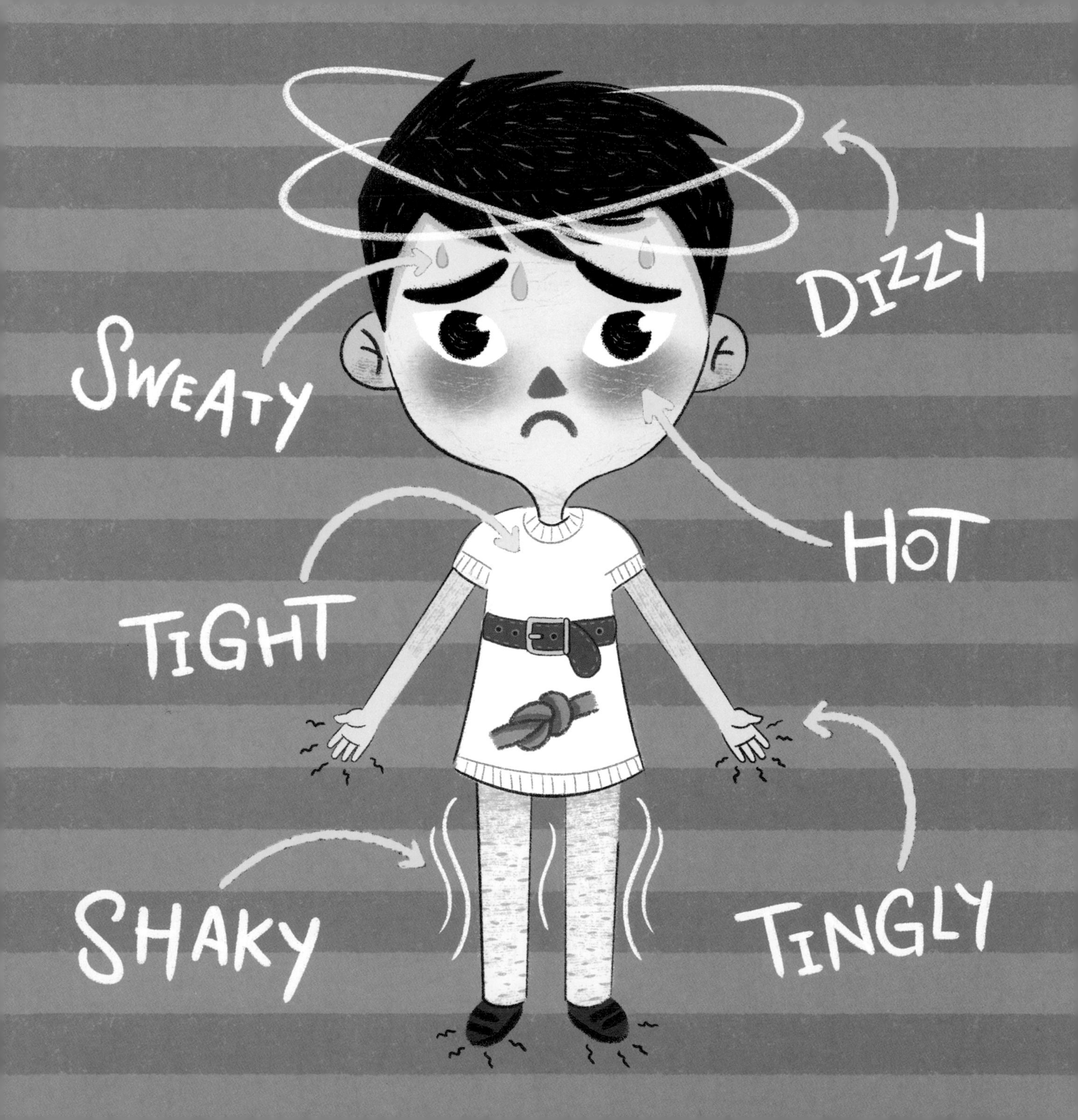
DIZZY
SWEATY
HOT
TIGHT
SHAKY
TINGLY

Even though it doesn't feel good,
it's OK to feel anxious.

Everyone feels anxious sometimes...

When we feel anxious,
it is important to know that
we can help our brains
and bodies calm down.

We can handle whatever
is making us feel this way.

If something specific is making you feel anxious or worried, it can be helpful to *identify* what that thing is.

Then you can figure out why it's making you feel anxious.

Once you have figured out
why you feel anxious, then
you can come up with a list of
solutions and pick the best one.

Worry:
School play
Why I'm Worried:
Don't have lines memorized yet
Solutions:
1. Cry on bed
2. Practice hard until I know them by heart
3. Draw a picture
4. Complain to parents
5. Bite nails

But sometimes when we feel anxious there isn't a problem to solve...

When this happens, try focusing your attention on something else.

You can use your **5 senses** to help notice what's happening right now, in the present moment.

Taste

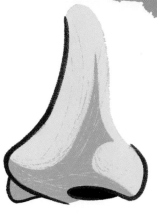

Smell

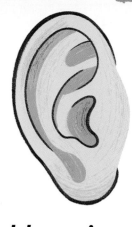

Hearing

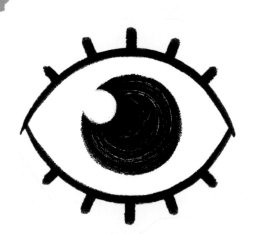

Sight

Touch

Start with your sense of **hearing.**
Get comfortable, close your eyes,
and try paying attention to
all of the sounds around you.

If you listen carefully, you can hear sounds up close and far away...

Sounds that are loud and sounds that are quiet...

Sounds that keep going and sounds that happen only once...

Sit for a few minutes and listen to what you can hear.

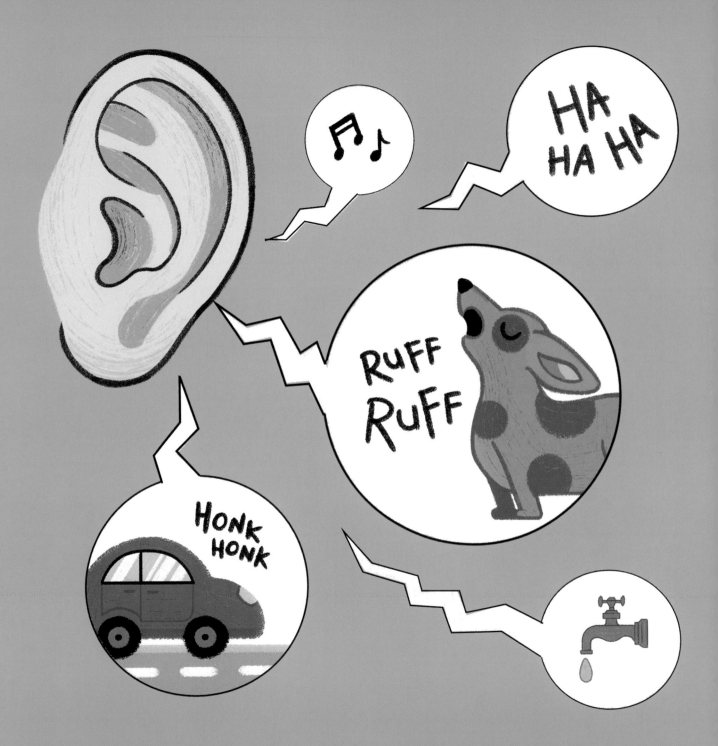

Another thing to do
when you feel anxious is
to **look** around you and
try to spot everything
that is your favorite color.

You can do this in your home,
in the car, at school, or outside.

Try to keep looking for things
that are your favorite color
until you feel a little calmer.

You can also use your **mind**
to do something that takes
a little bit of brain power.

Try singing a favorite song,
doing connect-the-dots, or
playing an alphabet naming game.

The anxious thoughts
may still be in your head...

But that's **OK!**
You can choose to focus on
something else instead.

The more you practice
handling your anxiety,
the easier it will become.

Remember...
Everyone feels anxious sometimes!

Claim Your FREE Gift!

Visit ➡ PDICBooks.com/Gift

Thank you for purchasing

Everyone Feels Anxious Sometimes,

and welcome to the Puppy Dogs & Ice Cream family.

We're certain you're going to love the little gift
we've prepared for you at the website above.